Little Red Riding Hood
and the Wolf

Retold by Ruth Mattison • Illustrations by Tracy La Rue Hohn

PIONEER VALLEY EDUCATIONAL PRESS, INC.

Once upon a time
there was a little girl.
She lived with her mother
and father in a small house
near a big forest.
The little girl liked to wear
a red cape with a red hood,
so everyone called her
Little Red Riding Hood.

One day, Little Red Riding Hood's
mother said, "Please take
this basket with bread and honey
to your grandmother.
She is feeling ill."

Little Red Riding Hood nodded
and picked up the basket.

"Don't forget. Do not stop
and talk to strangers
on the way," said her mother.

Little Red Riding Hood
walked through the forest
to her grandmother's house.
On the way she met a wolf.

"Hello, little girl," said the wolf.
"Where are you going?"

"Hello," said Little Red Riding Hood.
She forgot that her mother
told her not to talk to strangers.
"I am taking this basket of bread
and honey to my grandmother,"
she told the wolf.
"She is feeling ill."

"I hope she feels better soon,"
said the wolf.

The wolf was very hungry.
He took a shortcut and got
to Grandmother's house first.
He knocked on the door.

"Who's there?" asked Grandmother.

"It is me, Little Red Riding Hood,"
said the wolf.

"Come in! Come in!"
called Grandmother.
Grandmother was very ill,
but when she saw the wolf,
she jumped out of bed
and locked herself in the closet.

The wolf found a nightgown
and cap. He put them on
and climbed into bed.

When Little Red Riding Hood
got to Grandmother's house,
she went right in.
She looked at her grandmother
in bed. "Oh, Grandmother,"
she said. "What big ears you have!"

"All the better to hear you with,"
said the wolf.

"Oh, Grandmother!"
said Little Red Riding Hood.
"What big eyes you have!"

"All the better to see you with,"
said the wolf.

"Oh, Grandmother,
what big teeth you have,"
said Little Red Riding Hood.

"All the better to eat you with!"
said the wolf, and he jumped
out of bed.

"Help! Help!"
called Little Red Riding Hood.
She ran out the door,
and the wolf ran after her.

A woodcutter was chopping wood
in the forest. He saw
the wolf running after
Little Red Riding Hood.

"Stop!" he called.
He put out his foot
and tripped the wolf.

"Now be off with you, Wolf,
and never come back,"
said the woodcutter.
"If you do, I will
chop you up with my ax."

The wolf got up and ran
into the forest and was never
seen again.

Grandmother came running
out of the house.
Little Red Riding Hood
hugged her. "Oh, Grandmother!
When I talked to the wolf
in the forest, he was so nice."

"Let that be a lesson then,"
said her grandmother.
"Never talk to strangers!"